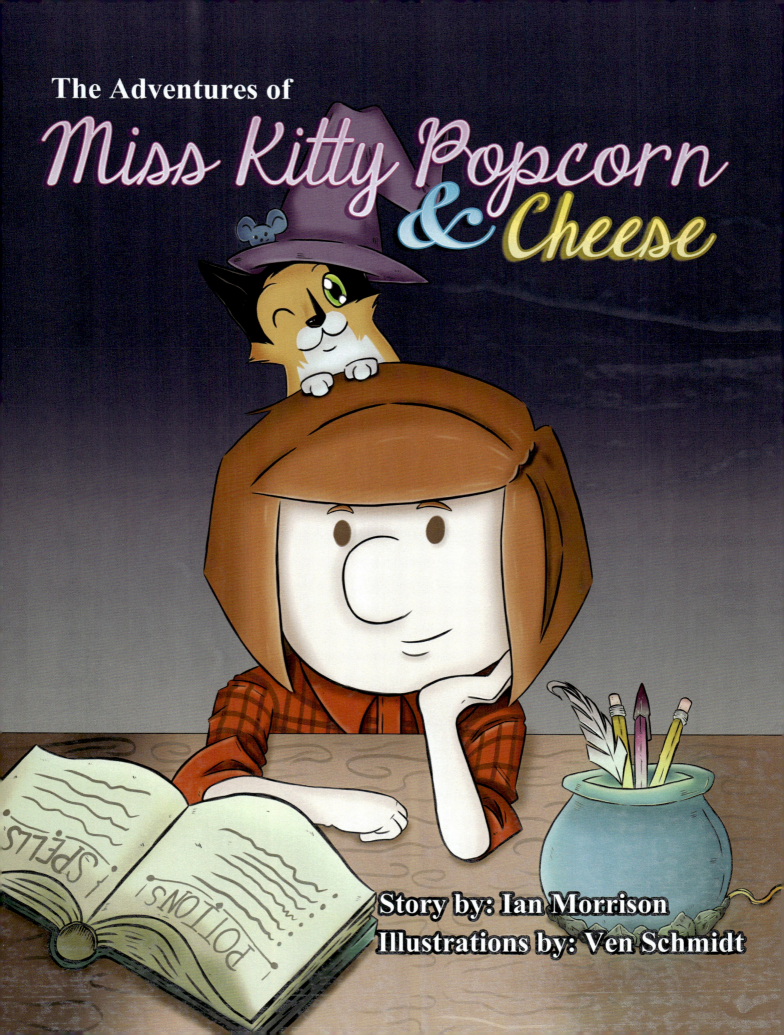

To order additional copies of this book, contact:
Xlibris
844-714-8691
www.Xlibris.com
Orders@Xlibris.com

ISBN: Softcover   978-1-7960-7809-1
         Hardcover   978-1-7960-7810-7
         EBook   978-1-7960-7808-4

Print information available on the last page

Rev. date: 04/19/2022

"To all things kitty, cheesy, and glittery..."

Sam is a very special girl. She comes from a long line of magical women. They're witches.

But very kind and good witches. Sam lives with her mom Sondra, her grandmother Maggie, her two Aunts Penny and Sylvia, and her cat- Miss Kitty Popcorn.

Sam named her Miss Kitty Popcorn because Miss Kitty LOVES popcorn.

She would eat it all the time if she could.

Miss Kitty Popcorn is a very special cat and follows Sam around to keep an eye on her for the family.

Miss Kitty Popcorn has a friend. A little mouse named Cheese. His name is Cheese because he only eats cheese! Miss Kitty Popcorn decided she did not want to chase mice like other cats.

She knew it was wrong to bully something just because it is smaller than her.

Like all witches in her family, Sam has to go to magic school. Sam doesn't like to wear the school dresses that all of the girls at magic school have to wear. Sam wants to wear what she wants to, and dress like the boys at her school. Sam also likes to do boy things.

She likes to play sports and wear shorts and tank tops and boy sneakers. Her mother, her Grandmother, and her two Aunts think that's just fine.

The semester at witch school seemed to last very long for Sam and she missed her family while she was at school.

She missed watching her Mother, her Grandmother, and her two Aunts perform magic spells around the house.

Also, the other girls at magic school weren't very nice.

Some of the witches in Sam's class would make fun of Sam because she likes to dress like a boy and do boy things - except for one other witch.

Her name is Brittany. Sam thinks she's pretty and likes her a lot.

All the women in Sam's family were very powerful witches. Sam wasn't very good at being a witch, and the other girls at school would bully her. They would tease Sam and say that Sam is a boys name.

The most popular girl at school, Nancy, would often bully Sam and play magical tricks on her. Sometimes Nancy would turn Sam's lunch invisible or make her juice boxes float and the other girls would just laugh.

Brittany would stick up for Sam and share her lunch with Sam when Nancy would play her magical tricks. Brittany liked the way Sam dressed and thought Sam was pretty.

During spell class, the teacher Miss Fine asked all of the students to cast a spell from the school's Big Book of Spells for the class midterms.

Sam wanted to fit in and be like the other girls, so she found a spell to make her be the best witch she could be.

Maybe wearing dresses and liking boys would make things easier.

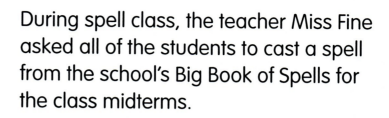

Sam put Miss Kitty Popcorn's food down and some cheese for Cheese. Sam then put her ingredients into the cauldron one by one and cast her spell.

Miss Kitty and Cheese were so excited to see Sam cast her big spell!

But nothing happened. Sam went over the spell to make sure she did everything right.

She even checked the Big Book of Spells a third time and could not figure out what went wrong.

Sam felt really sad and disappointed, and decided to take a nap. Maybe after some rest she could figure out what went wrong.

So Sam went to her room to nap and Miss Kitty Popcorn and Cheese stayed behind to finish their lunch.

Then something happened! The food in front of Miss Kitty Popcorn and Cheese started to glow!

Not noticing, Miss Kitty Popcorn and Cheese kept eating their popcorn and cheese.

After their food started glowing, it tasted like the best popcorn and cheese ever!

"Wow this is the best popcorn ever!" said Miss Kitty Popcorn.

Then Miss Kitty Popcorn realized something - she could talk!

"Hey I can talk!" she said.

"Cheese!" said Cheese.

"Cheese cheese cheese cheese cheese!"

Cheese was all that Cheese could say. But Miss Kitty Popcorn could understand every word!

Sam's spell must have done something to the food that Miss Kitty Popcorn and Cheese ate while it sat next to the cauldron.

Miss Kitty Popcorn and Cheese felt MAGICAL!

And they started doing magical things! They were having so much fun!

Even in all this excitement, Miss Kitty Popcorn and Cheese felt sad for Sam and wanted to help her get her proper grade in witch class.

So they needed a plan. They flew to Sam's room and saw Sam was upset.

"I'm a terrible witch." Sam cried.

"I hate this school, I hate this dress!"

Miss Kitty Popcorn and Cheese felt just as sad as Sam.

After her nap, Sam went back to her desk and her cauldron.

She tried to retrace the steps to her spell once again.

"I wonder what went wrong?" Sam asked herself.

"I wish the spell worked. I would have made myself a pretty dress to fit in with the other girls."

Miss Kitty Popcorn and Cheese overheard Sam's wish and used their magic to make a gorgeous new flannel dress for Sam.

Sam looked down at the new dress she had on and shouted,

"Oh my! The spell actually worked! I made a pretty dress!"

Sam thought her spell had finally kicked in, and did not know it was Miss Kitty Popcorn and Cheese performing the magic spell.

Then Sam looked at the dolls she has on her desk.

"I am done with these girly dolls! I wish they were fun, sporty things I would actually play with!"

Miss Kitty Popcorn and Cheese used their magic to turn Sam's dolls into soccer balls, a baseball bat, and all kinds of fun toys!

Sam was so proud of herself, thinking that her spell had worked.

The other students noticed how happy she was, smiling from ear to ear.

They saw that Sam could make anything happen that she wanted to!

They did not know it was Miss Kitty Popcorn and Cheese using their magic to perform all of the spells.

Sam was becoming very popular at school. She walked proudly down the halls, holding hands with her new girlfriend Brittany.

The next day at school, Nancy was the first witch called by Miss Fine to perform her midterm spell in front of the class.

Now Nancy had the Big Book of Spells by her cauldron at her desk.

"I'm going to conjure up the most magnificent unicorn anyone has ever seen!" Nancy bragged.

But Nancy never took the time to study her spells, she was too concerned with being the most popular witch at school.

Nancy hurried through her spell. She did not measure her ingredients and she was spilling stuff all over her desk and her cauldron.

"Maybe Nancy should have spent more time studying and less time bullying." Miss Kitty Popcorn said to Cheese.

"Cheese!" said Cheese to Miss Kitty Popcorn, and they both laughed to each other.

Suddenly, the cauldron started to shake and a big cloud formed over Nancy's desk.

When the smoke cleared, the class started to see something crawl out of the cauldron.

Instead of a beautiful unicorn, there appeared ...

A giant troll! Miss Fine grabbed her wand and approached the troll.

Before Miss Fine could cast any spell, the troll locked eyes with Miss Fine and turned her into stone!

Now the girls were really frightened with their teacher unable to help them, and started to panic.

"Sam you have to do something!" the girls shouted.

"You have to help us!"

Sam knew she needed to use her new magic to make this troll go away and turn Miss Fine back to normal. But Sam did not have any magic of her own, all of the magic she has been doing has come from Miss Kitty Popcorn and Cheese.

Miss Kitty Popcorn looked at Cheese and said,

"We have to help Sam and the girls! But what do we do?"

Cheese looked up at Miss Kitty Popcorn and just said "Cheese!".

Miss Kitty Popcorn and Cheese knew they would need to consult the big book of spells to defeat the troll.

But before they could act, Sam grabbed the book with Brittany, and they both ran back to Sam's desk to hide.

Sam and Brittany hid under her desk. Sam began looking through the Big Book of Spells for a way to banish the troll.

While skimming through the pages, some of the liquid from her cauldron was dripping onto the book.

Sam went to wipe the glowing liquid off the book and got a paper cut.

Sam put her finger in her mouth to try and stop her finger from bleeding, accidentally putting the glowing liquid into her mouth.

Sam's finger then started to glow just like the popcorn and cheese!

22

Miss Kitty Popcorn and Cheese saw what had happened. "I get it now!" said Miss Kitty Popcorn to Cheese.

"Sam's spell actually did work! But you have to eat or drink the potion from the cauldron for the spell to work! I ate the popcorn, and you ate the cheese. Sam ate some of the potion off of her finger!

Now Sam will have the same magical powers that we have!"
"Cheese cheese cheese!" said Cheese.

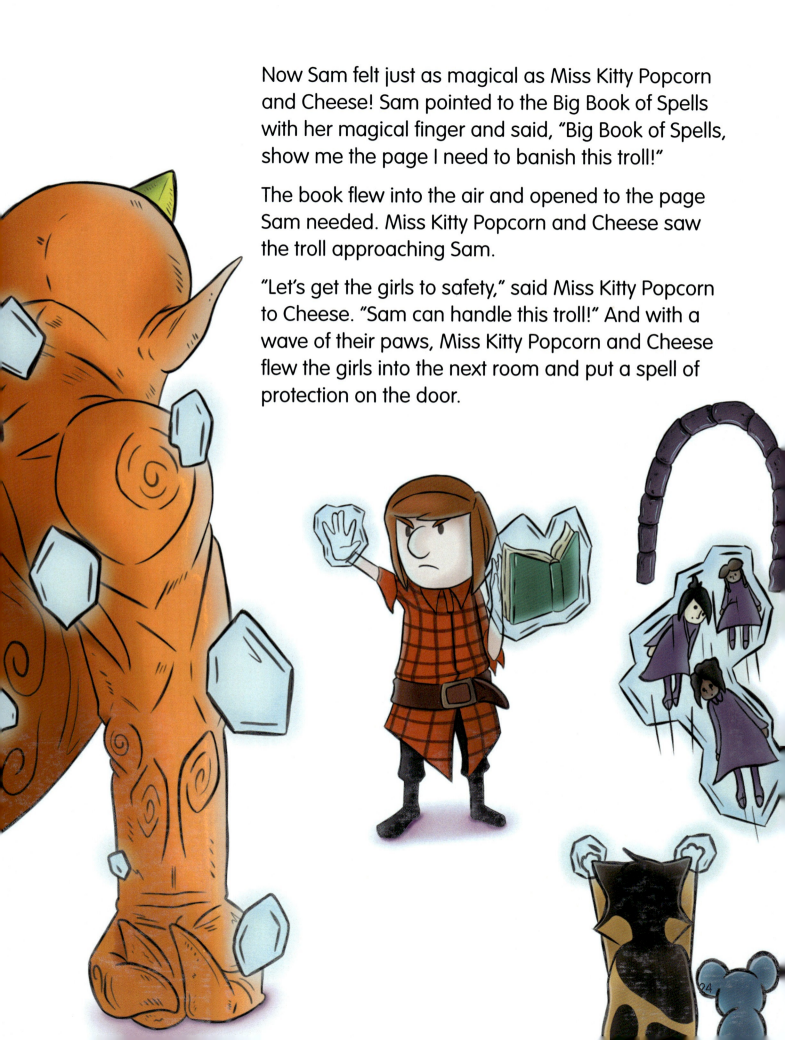

Now Sam felt just as magical as Miss Kitty Popcorn and Cheese! Sam pointed to the Big Book of Spells with her magical finger and said, "Big Book of Spells, show me the page I need to banish this troll!"

The book flew into the air and opened to the page Sam needed. Miss Kitty Popcorn and Cheese saw the troll approaching Sam.

"Let's get the girls to safety," said Miss Kitty Popcorn to Cheese. "Sam can handle this troll!" And with a wave of their paws, Miss Kitty Popcorn and Cheese flew the girls into the next room and put a spell of protection on the door.

Sam bravely stood up and started to read from the Big Book of Spells.
The troll disappeared into a big cloud of smoke. Sam could hear the
girls cheering from the other room.

"I knew she could do it!" said Miss Kitty Popcorn
to Cheese.

"Cheese cheese cheese!" said Cheese.

Sam used her magic to turn Miss Fine back to normal while Miss Kitty Popcorn and Cheese brought the girls back to the classroom.

Everyone gathered around Sam and cheered and thanked Sam for saving the day. Brittany proudly stood next to her girlfriend Sam and gave her a kiss on the cheek. Even Nancy came over to thank Sam and apologize.

"Thank you Sam." Nancy said.

"I'm sorry for how I treated you. I was mean to you because you were different, but now I see that being different makes you special.

I hope we can be friends". "Of course we can." said Sam. "Now let's help you get that unicorn spell right."

Together, Sam and Nancy created the most beautiful unicorn the school has ever seen.

Miss Fine loved the teamwork and gave both Sam and Nancy an A for the semester.

Sam quickly became close friends with all of the girls in her class.

The girls no longer made fun of Sam, and they were happy to see her and Brittany together!

When Sam returned home from witch school, the whole family was so proud to see how much Sam had changed.

Sam was no longer the shy and unhappy little witch she was before witch school. Sam was always smiling, always having fun, and was able to join the rest of the family in casting spells around the house.

Mom, Grandmom, the two Aunts, and Sam created a magical fruit tree so they could bake their new friends fruit pies all year round.

Miss Kitty Popcorn and Cheese were filled with joy watching the whole family grow closer than ever.

They were both excited for all of the magical adventures they were going to have with their new powers, with each other, and with Sam and Brittany.

The next semester of witch school was going to be the best one ever!

Miss Kitty Popcorn and Cheese both knew none of this would not have been possible if it wasn't for Sam.

They decided to keep their magic powers secret ... for now ...

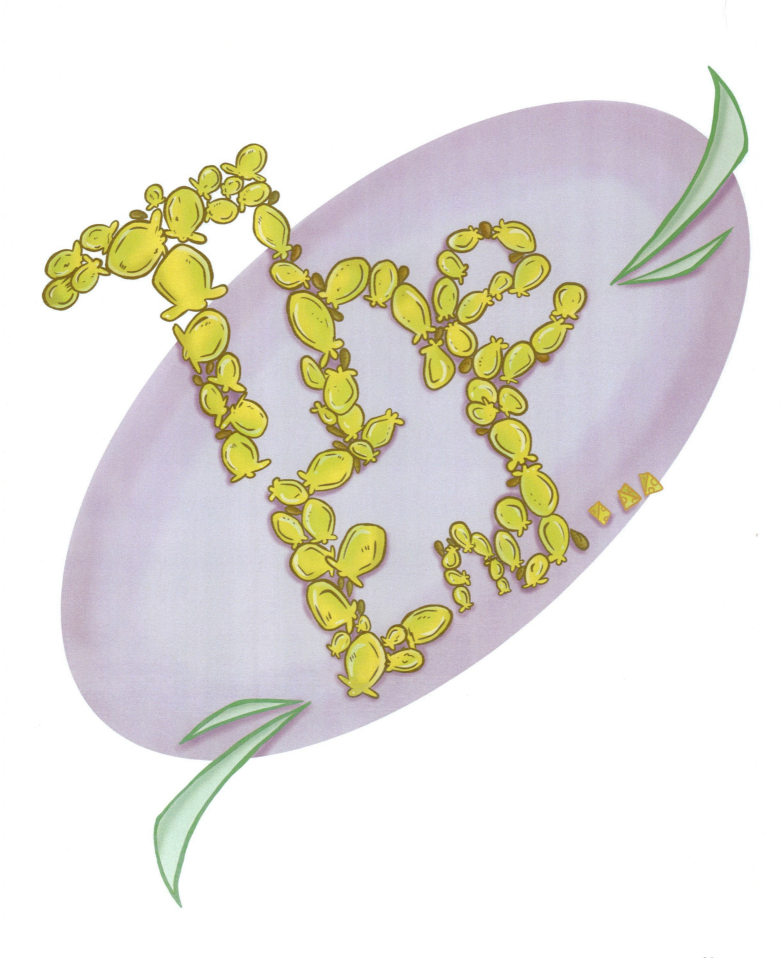